This book is dedicated to Auntie Zoe
who is so nice, so cool, so stylish
and SO like me.

EGMONT

First published in paperback in Great Britain 2013
by Egmont UK Limited
The Yellow Building, 1 Nicholas Road, London W11 4AN

Text copyright © 2013 Kjartan Poskitt
Illustrations copyright © 2013 David Tazzyman

The moral rights of the author and illustrator have been asserted

ISBN 978 1 4052 6271 2

1 3 5 7 9 10 8 6 4 2

www.egmont.co.uk

A CIP catalogue record for this title is available from the British Library

Printed and bound in Great Britain by the CPI Group (UK) Ltd, Croydon, CR0 4YY

51469/1

MIX
Paper
FSC FSC® C018306

EGMONT LUCKY COIN

Our story began over a century ago, when seventeen-year-old
Egmont Harald Petersen found a coin in the street.

He was on his way to buy a flyswatter, a small hand-operated
printing machine that he then set up in his tiny apartment.

The coin brought him such good luck that today Egmont has
offices in over 30 countries around the world. And that lucky
coin is still kept at the company's head offices in Denmark.

Agatha Parrot

and the **Heart of Mud**

Typed out neatly by
Kjartan Poskitt

Illustrated by David Tazzyman

EGMONT

The gang!

Bianca has got a secret supply of sweets hidden in her trombone case.

Martha got kissed by a **boy** once when she scored a goal at football!

Agatha (that's me). My record for the most number of holes in my tights is 17. And that's true.

Ivy showed her cat how to use the cat flap and got her head stuck.

Ellie only has one glove because she knitted it and then ran out of wool.

ODD STREET

No 1
Bianca

No 3
Martha

No 5
Agatha

No 7
Ivy

No 9
Ellie

CONTENTS

CONTENTS

The Heart of... *What?*

....

Hiya! I'm Agatha Jane Parrot and THANKS for reading this book. It's very nice of you because the title is a bit strange!

If you want to know why this book is called *The Heart of Mud*, it's something that somebody says later on in the story. If you like, you can flick through the pages and see if you can spot who says it. Remember you're on page 2 now, so I'll wait here and you can come back when you've found it.

I'll just hum some waiting music . . . *Tum-tee-tiddly-tum!*

If you think the title is a bit silly,

it could have been a LOT worse. There's one bit in the story where my friend Ivy sends secret messages with her leg! It's true, she really does, so Ivy wanted this book to be called *Ivy Malting and Her Secret-Message-Sending Leg* ha ha! But it was a bit long to fit on the front, so we used that name for one of the chapters instead.

Before we start, I should warn you that this book does have a bit of LOVE in it. (That's why it has *Heart* in the title.)

Don't worry. There's no long kissing or holding hands or anything gross like that. YUK! We don't do that sort of thing on Odd Street – apart from once. It was Dad's birthday so Mum had to give him a kiss, but they didn't like it much because he's bald and she's got hairy legs. What a pity Mum couldn't take the hairs off her legs and plant them

4

on Dad's head eh? That would have been a **brilliant** birthday present for him. How very thoughtful.

Anyway, Ivy's leg is waiting for you so we better get on with the story. WAHOO!

The Return of the Mud Creature

· ·

I n our house, Wednesday teatime is the BEST teatime of the week.

What makes Wednesday so good is that Mum cooks up 'A Real Taste of Italy'. It's made with fresh pasta and hand-picked tomatoes with an

6

exciting blend of herbs and covered with a rich cheese sauce. Each serving also contains 377 calories, 13 grams of fat and 832 mg of sodium (whatever that means).

How do I know all this? Because that's what it says on the box. YUM!

We love teatime out of boxes. Even Dad can't cook it wrong, apart from the time when he forgot to poke holes in the top with a fork and it went BADDOOF in the microwave.

The smell lasted for weeks! Mum went mental with him, but secretly she was dead pleased because when her friends came round they thought she'd been cooking some posh stuff like they do on telly.

'What IS that lovely smell?' said the friends.

'It's my new secret recipe,' said Mum the Big Fibber.

Gosh if I told whoppers like that, I'd be straight up to bed with no arguing.

The bad thing is that we can only have box tea on Wednesdays, because Wednesday is the only day when there are four of us for tea. The box says *serves four* and WE MUST OBEY the box.

So anyway, one Wednesday we were all sitting round the table waiting for our exciting herbs and 13 grams of fat. The four of us were Mum, Dad, me and little sister Tilly. As usual, Tilly was dressed as a fairy

9

and she was watching the numbers on the microwave count down so she could do her magic spell at the end.

'Five, four, three two, one . . .' said the fairy then she waved her wand.

PING! went the microwave oven.

Dad got the plastic box thing out and peeled the top back. *Oh wow, smell that smell, love it love it.* He was just dolloping it out on to four plates when we heard an evil scraping

sound coming from outside.

The front gate squeaked and the scraping sound got closer, and then the front door burst open. A hideous creature covered in mud staggered into the hallway leaving a slimy trail all over the mat.

'UM OME!' wailed the creature.

'Oh no!' said me and Tilly. The last thing we had wanted to see was the Mud Creature from Planet Smelly, but there it was.

The Mud Creature had been playing football. Usually he had tea at his friend Matty's house on Wednesdays but obviously something had gone wrong.

'UM OME!' he said again.

'What's he saying?' asked Dad.

'He says "I'm home",' said Mum, then she shouted into the hallway. 'Don't come in the kitchen like that.'

'Like what?' said the creature.

'Like THAT!' snapped Mum.

'You'll have to get undressed in the hall.'

By now you've probably guessed that the Mud Creature from Planet Smelly is actually my big brother James. This was not good news for me and Tilly. We started shovelling the pasta inside us as fast as we could because we knew what was coming next.

'Did you get tea at Matty's?' asked Dad.

'No,' said the Creature. 'He wasn't playing today.'

Dad went to the cupboard to get another plate out.

Shovel shovel shovel went me and Tilly.

'Wait, you two,' said Dad. 'We'll need to save a bit for James.'

And sure enough Dad spooned a HUGE bit off both our plates and plonked it on a plate for the Mud Creature. UNFAIR. I just hope

James got all my 13 grams of fat in his bit. It would have served him right.

After we had eaten our SMALL HELPINGS of box tea, Dad stood up and pulled an important face.

'I'll leave you people to clear up. I've got a bit of work to do in my office.'

Office? That sounds grand doesn't it? I bet you're thinking that Dad's office has a big desk with lots of telephones and a giant window with helicopters outside.

Actually it's not quite like that surprise surprise gosh faint in shock.

There's a cupboard in the corner of our living room, and one of the shelves has the computer on it. You have to get a kitchen chair and sit with your knees in the bottom of the cupboard and your bottom sticking out blocking the telly. That's Dad's office! No big desk and no helicopters.

Aw shame! Let's all weep for Dad
boo hoo hoo.

While Dad clicked his computer
on, Mum went to tidy up the hallway.
James fetched his football kit and
plonked it by the washing machine,
but when he thought Mum wasn't
looking, he dumped a huge muddy
rag in the bin. I couldn't resist having
a look and giving it a poke.

'What's that?' I asked.

'Shhh!' grinned James. 'It's

Martha's football shirt.'

'It's ripped to bits!' I said.

'I know. She didn't want her mum to see it.'

I wasn't surprised.

Martha lives next door at number 3 and she's brilliant because she's big and jolly. Martha's mum is like an even bigger and jollier version of Martha apart from sometimes when she isn't jolly, and that's usually when Martha has been playing football. Martha likes a bit of pushing and shoving, so when the boys try to tackle her, it all gets a bit lively. I've seen her knock three over at once, and then drag them along the ground while they cling on to her shirt. **WAHOO** GO MARTHA!

It was a nice little bit of excitement having Martha's old shirt secretly hiding in our bin, but another even MORE exciting bit of excitement happened next.

Dad stuck his head in the doorway. 'James, you've got an email,' he said.

'Me?' said James. 'Who from?'

'Ho ho!' said Dad. 'It's a secret admirer.'

WHAT?

WOOO-HOOO!

Whizz . . . rush . . . zoom!

About half a second later all five of us were jammed round the computer.

This is what the message said:

Dear James,

How do you do? I am your cousin Bella. Granny and Grandad say that you are the same age as me so I am just writing to say hello. I like theatre and dancing. What are your hobbies?

Please email me back.

Love from Bella.

James pulled a face. 'Who IS this?' he said.

'Your cousin,' said Dad. 'She's your Auntie Zoe's girl.'

Oh wow! Auntie Zoe is the coolest person in our family. I've never actually met her*, but I can tell you exactly what she looks like. She's really tall and slim with big eyes and short black hair. How do I know? Because she models dresses in *The Duchess Catalogue* that Mum reads!

the Dudess

(* Actually Dad says I did meet Auntie Zoe once. I was very small and sitting on her knee when she was wearing a light blue dress, and my nappy was leaking a bit EEEK! So we'll ignore that one, and just say that I've never met her. The point is that Auntie Z is a model and I'm going to be a model too, so we're soulmates. Yahoo fab.)

Dad stood up and made us all shuffle round so that James could sit down at the computer.

'What am I supposed to do?' moaned James.

'You'll send her a nice reply,' said Mum. 'We never see Zoe's family these days. It's very kind of Bella to get in touch.'

'But she put LOVE FROM

26

BELLA on the end,' moaned James. 'I'm not having any of that!'

'She was just being friendly,' said Dad. 'Now get on with it.'

We all stood round James waiting for him to type something, but all he did was blush bright red. Ha ha love it!

'Do you MIND?' snapped James. 'This is private!'

So we all had to move away and leave him to it which was a bit boring.

Never mind. The fact was that James had got LOVE from a MYSTERY GIRL so I had to rush out and tell all my friends.

It's one of those things that sisters have to do.

The Best of
Enemies

•••••••••••••••••••••••••••••••••

I opened our front door and EEEK there was Martha standing there about to whack me on the nose!

Actually she wasn't, she was just reaching out to ring the doorbell, but you know what it's like when you open the door and somebody's already there. (Martha's the one I told you about who lives next door at number 3.)

'Hey Martha,' I said. I couldn't wait to tell her about James getting some LOVE from somebody. 'You'll never guess what's happened!'

'Mum's stopped me from playing football,' said Martha.

'No, that's not it,' I said.

'Yes, it IS it!' said Martha.

Then I realised she wasn't joking. She looked really fed up.

'Is it because of your shirt?' I asked.

Martha nodded. 'Partly that. But mainly what SHE said.'

Martha walked back out to the street and pointed at the little fence in front of her house. Ivy was balancing on the top, practising tightrope walking. (Ivy is the mad one who lives at number 7.)

'I said I was sorry,' said Ivy. 'It just came out.'

'What came out?' I asked.

Martha explained. Basically, when she got back from football, her mum opened the door and saw she was just wearing her vest under her coat. Her mum had gone nuts about the football shirt and did one of those BIG TALKS that mums do from time to time. In the end she said that Martha could only have another football shirt if she got on to the school spelling team.

'The *spelling* team?' I gasped. 'What's that got to do with football?'

'Mum said if I had to do sport, why couldn't I do something less messy?' said Martha.

'And I just happened to be going past . . .' said Ivy.

'No you didn't,' snapped Martha. 'You came out to listen to me getting told off!'

'All I said was, "What about the spelling team"?' said Ivy who was still walking along the fence. 'Mrs Twelvetrees is starting a spelling club and they're going to have a school team.'

'Spelling is NOT a proper sport!' moaned Martha.

'Why not?' said Ivy. 'It's a team, like a football team.'

'But I'll never get on the spelling team!' said Martha.

'I was only being helpful,' said Ivy. 'It's not my fault you're rubbish at spelling.'

Martha grabbed the fence with both hands and wobbled it. Ivy fell off and bashed her knee on the pavement which made it bleed. They both looked at me crossly to see whose side I was on.

'There's only one answer,' I said. 'Why don't you BOTH go along to spelling club?'

'BOTH?' they both said.

'Martha will have to go anyway, but Ivy got you into it. The least Ivy can do is help you get on the team.'

Ivy gave her knee a lick. 'OK,' she said.

Martha looked at Ivy in surprise. 'Do you mean it?'

'Of course,' said Ivy. 'If that's what you want.'

Martha reached down and helped Ivy up. 'Nasty bash on your

37

knee,' she said. 'Sorry about that.'

'It'll look great in the morning,' giggled Ivy.

'Yeah, all blue and scabby!' laughed Martha. 'Hey, have a look at what I did playing football.'

So Martha showed Ivy her knee and DING they were friends again.

Then I remembered that I was going to tell them about James and the *Love from Bella* message, but they were having so much fun with their knees, I decided I'd tell them later.

Instead I went in to see how lover boy had been getting on.

Nice and Friendly and Boring

....

When I got into the living room, James was at the computer with Dad looking over his shoulder.

'Come on, James,' said Dad. 'You can do better than that!'

'But I don't want to do this stupid

email,' said James crossly.

'Why not?'

'Because I don't even know this Bella and she put LOVE on the end!'

'So?'

'So she's a weirdo!' said James. 'Why does she think she loves me? That's gross! And now Agatha's laughing at me.'

'No she isn't,' said Dad being very serious.

Yes she was actually. I was

trying to keep a straight face but I couldn't help it, and neither could Dad. In fact he was trying so hard not to laugh, his nose suddenly did a big squeaky squirt.

HA HA HA HA HA!

James ran out of the room and slammed the door.

'Poor old James,' giggled Dad. 'But we can't send this. Your mum will go mad. Look.'

So I looked.

hey bella, h8 theter and h8
dansin. hobis = fball i support
ROVERS 4 eva. J

(If you can't understand it, don't
worry. It took me a few goes, and in
the end it wasn't worth it.)

Dad was right. Mum would go
mad if that message got sent. What
was worse is that maybe Auntie Zoe
would go mad too and I didn't want
that. When I leave school and start

to be a model, I might need Auntie Zoe to give me a few tips like what face I have to pull when I'm having my photo taken. But what if James's message made Auntie Zoe fall out with us? It could ruin all my plans for future greatness. EEEK!

'Why don't I write a message?' I said. 'I'll pretend it's from James and make it nice and friendly.'

'But what if Bella writes back?' said Dad.

44

'Don't worry,' I said. 'She won't!'

It always takes me ages to type on a computer, because I like inventing little sideways faces. Here's somebody trying to lick their nose (:-9) ha ha! But I did this message really smartly with CAPITAL LETTERS and everything. Here's how it started.

Dear Bella,

Thank you for your message.

I am a very boring person. I do
not like any of the things you like.
And my only hobby is

What was the most boring thing
I could think of? And then I
remembered Ivy and Martha
fighting and thought of the
PERFECT thing! After that, the only
problem was dealing with the
Love from bit. Hmmm . . . James
was right. It's a bit much to be

LOVING somebody when you
don't actually know them. But it
must be all right to LIKE them.
That seemed fair enough. Here's
how the whole message looked:

Dear Bella,

Thank you for your message.
I am a very boring person. I do
not like any of the things you like.
And my only hobby is spelling.
I think spelling is really good

fun. So you won't be wanting to send me any more emails.

Like from James.

P.S. Tell Auntie Zoe that Agatha is very pretty and is going to be a model too {;-)

I'd just finished typing it out when Dad came in and looked over my shoulder.

'Clever!' he said. 'But we better get it sent before James sees it.'

So he clicked SEND and that was the end of that.

(Actually you must have realised that this book has loads more pages, so of course that wasn't the end of that.)

Welcome to the Club

· ·

The next thing to sort out was getting Martha and Ivy on to this spelling team thing. We'd all got a letter home about it and mine was still in the bottom of my school bag.

I went to the hall, got the bag off

50

the peg, opened it up, shut my eyes,

stuck my hand in

and hoped

for the best.

It's a bit like

a lucky dip, but

more of a YUKKY

dip ha ha! Here are

some of the lovely prizes

I pulled out:

One leaky pen with hair

stuck to it.

One old
biscuit wrapper
with hair stuck
to it.

One hair bobble all
knotted up with hair stuck
to it.

One comb
covered in
jam from a random
sandwich with
hair stuck to it.

52

And finally – *TA DAH!* –

One crumpled-up letter smeared in chocolate with hair stuck to it.

I put all the other stuff back (because that's where it lives) and opened up the letter.

The new spelling club will meet at lunchtimes. There will be a weekly test, and the best four pupils will be selected for the Odd Street School Spelling Team! The team will compete with other schools to win books for the library.

My my, what jolly fun.

At the bottom of the letter was a permission slip which you had to tear off and fill in if you wanted to join the club.

The next morning, we were all outside school waiting for Motley the caretaker to open up the doors. I made sure that Martha and Ivy had their slips filled in. Ellie and Bianca came over to see what was going on,

so I asked if they wanted to have a
go too.

'Ooh not me,' said Ellie. 'Spelling
tests are really scary!'

'What's to be scared of?' I said.

'I had a bad dream about a
spelling test once. I had to spell all
these different words but I was only
allowed to use the letter g.'

Poor Ellie. Everything scares her,
but Bianca's a lot braver. Maybe
she'd have a go?

'I better not,' said Bianca. 'I'm not very good at welling spurds.'

'*Welling spurds?*' we all said. We love Bianca. Don't always understand her but love her.

'Oh I get it!' said Ellie. 'She means SPELLing WORDs!'

'That's right,' said Bianca. 'I get the metters all lixed up.'

By this time Ivy was running round the playground with her permission slip hanging out of her mouth like a long tongue. She ended up bashing into Gwendoline Tutt and Olivia Livid who are in the other class from us. Gwendoline lives in a really posh house at the top end of Odd Street, and Olivia is her evil slave who probably lives in a cave somewhere and chews bones for tea. They're both really unpopular, so it's no wonder that nobody likes them.

Typical Olivia snatched Ivy's slip out of her mouth and read it.

'What is that?' demanded Gwendoline.

'Ivy's joining the spelling club!' laughed Olivia.

'*Spelling club?*' repeated Gwendoline. She took the slip from Olivia and read it. 'LOSERS club, more like! I wouldn't be seen dead doing that.'

'It's going to be brilliant actually,' said Ivy. 'Loads of people are doing it!'

'Oh yeah?' said Gwendoline. 'Who else is a big loser?'

We all looked at Martha, but Martha just kicked the ground and kept quiet. Gwendoline threw the slip back at Ivy, then Gwendoline and Olivia wandered off laughing.

'I've changed my mind,' said Martha. She got her permission slip out of her pocket and looked around for the rubbish bin. 'I don't want to do it.'

'But then you'll never get to play football again!' I said.

'Have I got to do it if Martha doesn't?' asked Ivy.

'If Ivy doesn't then I'm definitely not,' said Martha.

Ooh, I hated Gwendoline Tutt sometimes! Well, most times actually.

'Give me those!' I said taking the slips off them. 'I'll hand them in so you BOTH know that you're BOTH doing it.'

Martha and Ivy looked a bit sulky.

'But what about Gwendoline

laughing at us?'

'Don't worry about Gwendoline,' I promised them. 'She won't be laughing for long.'

I dug my hand into my bag. It's lucky I'm organised! I'd put my spelling club letter back in along with all the other stuff and it still had a blank permission slip to tear off at the bottom. Ha ha – I knew just what to do!

When it got to playtime, I went

to hand the permission slips in to Miss Wizzit at reception. This sort of thing is never easy because it doesn't matter who you are or what you want, Miss Wizzit always makes it obvious that she's far too busy to help. You could be Queen Cleopatra with your pants on fire, but Miss Wizzit would still make you wait until she'd finished finding the end on the sellotape or polishing the photocopier.

Today she was in an extremely far-too-busy-for-anything mood because Miss Barking was hanging around watching her. Miss B is the deputy headteacher who has big square glasses like telly screens, and always carries a folder full of boring forms to fill in.

I don't know what Miss Barking wanted but whatever it was, she wasn't getting it. Miss Wizzit was madly stapling lots of things together

CHONK CHONK CHONK.

I had to waggle the permission slips at her for ages before she snatched them off me, banged a staple through them CHONK and chucked them in a drawer. At least it gave Miss Barking something to talk about.

'Miss Wizzit!' said Miss Barking. 'Those are permission slips.'

'I know,' said Miss Wizzit. 'But they're only for spelling club.'

'Only?' said Miss Barking.

'ONLY? You need to put all those names on the dangerous activity register.'

'Why?'

'Lunchtime . . . spellings . . . children . . . Isn't it obvious?'

Miss Wizzit shook her head.

'What if one of the children was injured with an over-sharpened pencil?' said Miss Barking. 'Or swallowed a book? Or got a finger trapped inside a piece of folded paper?'

MissWizzit wasn't impressed. 'I'm surprised I don't need a permission slip to use my stapler,' she muttered.

'You mean you haven't got one?' gasped Miss Barking. 'Stop at once!'

She hurried over and took Miss Wizzit's stapler off her. Then she opened up her folder and fumbled about for a *Stapler Usage in the Workplace* form or something daft like that.

Poor Miss Wizzit. She loved her

stapler but even she had to give in when Miss Barking was handing forms out.

Miss Wizzit snatched the slips back out of the drawer and flicked through them. 'Ivy Malting,' she said reading aloud. 'And Martha Swan. And . . . what's this?'

It was a third permission slip, but it was a bit hard to read because it was all crumpled and had a load of hair and chocolate stuck to it.

Miss Wizzit waved it in my face.

'Wizzit?' asked Miss Wizzit.

'It's Gwendoline Tutt,' I said.

'Gwendoline Tutt?' gasped Miss Wizzit. She pulled the sort of face that you can only pull if you're Miss Wizzit, and you've just found out that the most spoilt girl in the school wants to join the boring spelling club.

I smiled sweetly.

'She's spelling mad is Gwendoline. There's no stopping

the girl. Honest.'

And I toddled out of reception leaving Miss Wizzit still staring at the hairy permission slip.

My work was done. Tum-tee-tum. Diddly-dum.

What???

....

That evening Dad was being strange.

He didn't say much during tea, he just kept giving me funny looks and winking when nobody else was watching. Then, as soon as the others were out of the way, he called me into the living room and opened the cupboard door. His computer was already on, and there was an email on the screen.

Dear James,

THANK YOU FOR YOUR MESSAGE! I can't believe it! Spelling is my FAVOURITE thing too!!!! I hate theatre and dancing, I only said I liked them because my mum said it would make me sound more interesting. I am in the school spelling team and we practise every playtime. Today I got NECESSARY, POISONOUS and AUTOGRAPH all correct! What's your favourite word?

Love from Bella.

WHAT?????????

Zogs and Debras

· ·

I know that last chapter was a bit short, but nothing else happened. Dad had no idea what to do so we just zapped the email. Deleted it. Killed it. Trashed it. I mean, honestly, how could anyone reply to that? So, moving on . . .

It was lunchtime on the first day of spelling club. Mrs Twelvetrees was standing in the corridor outside the library. She's our headteacher with lots of lipstick and jangly necklaces.

'In you come, one and all!' she was calling out. 'Don't be shy, chaps, have a go!'

Me and Ivy and Martha were hanging around at the end of the corridor, and we had Ellie and Bianca with us too. So far, only three people had gone in. They were Hannah, Nicola and Andrew from James's class.

'They'll get on the team for sure,' said Martha. 'Those three eat books for breakfast. What chance have I got?'

'You'll be fine,' I said. 'The team has four people, so they need one more.'

'Come on Martha,' said Ivy. 'It's just a little spelling test. Let's get in there.'

Ivy took hold of Martha's sleeve and tried to pull her along, but Martha grabbed on to the radiator. Even with Bianca and Ellie pushing too, Martha wasn't going to budge.

'It's all right for you Ivy,' said Martha. 'You're good at spelling.'

'I promise I'll get them all wrong,' said Ivy.

'But I'll get them all wrong too,' said Martha. 'I know I will, and then I'll look stupid.'

'Don't worry Martha,' I said. 'It's the first week so it'll just be easy words.'

'Like zog and debra,' said Bianca.

'*Zog* and *debra*?' repeated Martha.

'She means DOG and ZEBRA!' I said. 'But Bianca's right. It's bound to be animals because they're easy. And they always ask for *zebra*, it makes you practise writing a z.'

'Maybe you'll get *cat* and *fish*,' said Ellie. 'Or *lion*. Or *sheep*.'

'I can spell animals!' said Martha.

She did a big smile and let go of the radiator.

'How about *rhinoceros?*' said Ivy. 'That's an animal. Or *hippopotamus?*'

'Eeek!' yelped Martha and she grabbed the radiator again.

'You won't get anything as hard as that!' I said. 'Mrs Twelvetrees won't want to scare people off.'

Martha took a deep breath and let go again.

'OK Ivy,' she said. 'Let's do it.'

They were setting off down the corridor when Gwendoline came by.

'Hello losers!' said Gwendoline. 'On your way to spelling club? Or is spelling a bit too exciting for you?'

Martha ran back and grabbed the radiator AGAIN.

'Well THANKS A LOT Gwendoline!' snapped Ivy as Gwendoline swaggered on past us.

'Relax,' I said. 'Watch this, Martha.'

Just as Gwendoline reached the library, Mrs Twelvetrees put on her biggest smile.

LIBRAR

'Ah Gwendoline!' gushed Mrs T. 'So glad you could make it.'

'What? Who?' said Gwendoline looking round, but there was nobody else there. And definitely nobody else called Gwendoline.

'Your father is so thrilled that you're joining our little club.'

'My father?' gasped Gwendoline. 'What makes him think I'm doing this?'

'I told him at the governors'

meeting,' said Mrs T. 'He's looking forward to you telling him all about it!'

What choice did Gwendoline have? In she went.

HA HA HA HA HA!

Ivy was hopping up and down in excitement.

'Come on Martha,' said Ivy. 'We can do this! Let's get in there and show Gwendoline how rubbish she really is!'

A big smile crept across Martha's face. 'Dog and zebra?' she asked me.

'Dog and zebra,' I assured her.

'Let's go!' said Martha.

'**YAHOO!**' shouted Ivy.

The two of them stuck their arms out like aeroplane wings then they charged down the corridor into the library and almost knocked Mrs Twelvetrees for six.

'Golly,' said Mrs Twelvetrees.

Me and Bianca and Ellie decided

to hang round and wait. We probably talked about something but I can't remember what, so here's a poem instead.

Tinky tonk
Tiddly plop
Tick tock
Went the clock

(OK, I admit it needs work, but at least it passed the time.)

LIMERICK COUNTY LIBRARY

The door opened again and Mrs Twelvetrees let everybody out.

'There,' said Mrs T. 'Wasn't that thrilling? I'll see you all next time!'

Out came Hannah, Nicola and Andrew looking jolly. Then Ivy and Martha came out NOT looking jolly. Finally Gwendoline shoved her way out between them.

'Ha ha losers,' said Gwendoline. 'You got them all wrong!'

'Big deal,' said Ivy. 'You only

88

got one right.'

'Then that beats you, doesn't it?' said Gwendoline. 'And I wasn't even trying.'

Off she went down the corridor, knocking into people and laughing.

'What happened?' I asked them.

'It's not like spelling in class,' moaned Ivy. 'To get on the team, you have to get three special star words right.'

'You said we'd get animals like

dog and *zebra*,' moaned Martha.

'Didn't you get *zebra*?' said Bianca. 'That's a shame. Zebras are wack and blight and they eat grots of lass.'

'I DON'T CARE!' snapped Martha.

(Poor Bianca! I'll put her zebra facts in at the back of the book to make up for it.)

'So what words did you get?' I asked.

'*Necessary*,' said Ivy.

'*Poisonous*,' said Martha.

'That's unfair!' I said. 'It's only the first week. I can't believe they made you spell *necessary* and *poisonous* and *autograph*.'

Suddenly they were all looking at me.

'*Autograph*?' gasped Martha.

'How did YOU know *autograph* was the other star word?' said Ivy.

It was a good question. How

DID I know? I was pulling my hair like mad. It's what I always do when I'm thinking to wake my brain up.

Then suddenly I remembered – those were the three long words that were in Bella's email. WOOOH SPOOKY!

There was only one possible explanation.

Bella's teacher must have been using the same lists of spelling words as Mrs T. They probably got them off some secret teacher page on the internet. The only difference was that Bella's teacher was a week ahead.

Ooooh . . . !

I must have had a big smile on my face because Martha prodded me crossly.

'What's so funny?' she demanded.

'I know how we can get you on the spelling team!'

Inside Information

······································

That night I told Dad I felt a bit mean about deleting Bella's message. He was surprised, but he said I could send her more messages so long as I kept them nice and friendly. So, nice and friendly it was then . . .

Dear Bella,

Thank you for telling me your words. We never get words like that. My hardest word was ZEBRA. Tell me what words you get next time, I'm really interested. Honest I am.

Like from James.

Then there was a day in between when nothing much happened (it was a bit of a 'Tinky Tonk Tiddly Plop'

day actually), but the next night
I got this:

> Dear James,
>
> I LOVE your messages! Today we got FOREIGN, ADDRESSES and SPAGHETTI. Tell me more about yourself. I've got long brown hair and I'm the tallest in my class. What do you look like?
>
> Lots of love from Bellz.

YAHOO! Good for Bella. I carefully copied the words out on to a piece of paper. It looked like this could work!

Ivy Malting and Her Secret-Message-Sending Leg

· ·

Next day at lunchtime we were all outside sitting on the bench. Martha and Ivy looked at the bit of paper I was holding. It had *foreign, addresses* and *spaghetti* on it.

'Are you sure those words are in the test?' said Martha.

'It's worth a try,' I said. 'But can you remember them, Martha?'

No she couldn't, was the simple answer to that. It was OK for Ivy, because she only had to say the letters out loud once to learn them. But Martha?

'F-O-R-R-I-N' said Martha.

'That's nothing like how you

spell *foreign*!' I said.

'Thank goodness for that,' said Martha. 'I was trying to spell *spaghetti*.'

HA HA HA HA HA!

We were glad Martha could joke about it, but how was she going to get the spellings right in the test?

'You could take that bit of paper in with you,' said Ivy.

'Too risky,' I said. 'Mrs Twelvetrees might see it.'

'Then you'd tree in big bubble,' said Bianca.

Bianca was right. And even though Mrs Twelvetrees is really nice, she is the headteacher, so you don't want to tree in big bubble with her.

'You need to write the words down somewhere less obvious,' I said.

'Martha could write them on the back of her hand,' said Ivy.

'Still a bit obvious,' I said.

'I suppose so,' said Ivy. Then she pulled her sock down to see how the scab on her knee was getting along . . . and accidentally gave me a brilliant idea!

'Hey Martha,' I said. 'When you did spellings, where did the two of you sit?'

'Ivy was on the table next to me,' said Martha. 'But there was a gap in between so we couldn't copy.'

'A gap?' I said. 'That's perfect.

So could you look down and see Ivy's legs?'

'Well, I could if I wanted to,' said Martha pulling a strange face. 'But why would I want to see Ivy's legs?'

Oh honestly! Do I have to explain EVERYTHING?

At least Ellie and Bianca had understood. Bianca got one of her thick art pens out of her bag, and then passed it over to Ellie who can do neat writing without any rubbing out.

Soon Ellie had written the three words in big letters on Ivy's leg, then Ivy pulled her sock up to cover them over. When it got to the spelling test, all Ivy had to do was pull her sock down and Martha could copy the words out. **Perfect!**

But then Gwendoline Tutt came marching over, looking smug.

'Are you two ready to lose again?' said Gwendoline. 'Because I've been practising

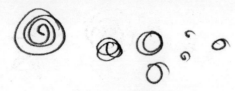

all this week.'

'Practising?' I said. 'Why do YOU
want to be on the spelling team?'

'My dad said he'll give me my
own laptop if I get on,' said
Gwendoline. 'A PINK one.'

'Then tough luck,' said Ivy.
'Because Martha will get on the
team, not you.'

'Martha?' said Gwendoline and
she did a horrible laugh. 'Are you
serious? I don't even know why she's

bothering.'

Gwendoline set off to go to spelling club. I was really wishing I hadn't put her name on that permission slip. Never mind, she was going to be in for a surprise!

Ivy had a look down inside her sock to make sure the words were still there, then she and Martha went in to spelling club too. Me and Ellie and Bianca waited outside like we did before.

Tinky tonk

Tiddly plop

Tick tock

Went the clock

(It might be rubbish, but you have to admit it's catchy.)

This time when the club had finished, Ivy and Martha came out with big happy faces.

'Ivy's leg worked perfectly,' said Martha. 'But how did you know what words it was going to be?'

'James's girlfriend told me,' I said.

'I didn't know James had a girlfriend,' said Martha.

'Neither does he!' I said.

They all gave me a funny look, but they knew it was better not to ask questions. The good news was that Martha had got the star words right! But there was also some bad news, and it was stomping down the corridor towards us.

'Well well well,' said Gwendoline.
'Fancy Martha getting them all
right!'

'You got two right,' said Martha
trying to be nice. 'So you did very
well.'

'Don't give me THAT!' said
Gwendoline. 'You were just lucky,
but next week I'll beat you and it'll
be ME on the team.'

Too Many Xs!

••••••••••••••••••••••••••

I love it when my plans work, so I couldn't wait to give it another go. All I had to do was send Bella a nice reply to her last message and get the star words for next week. There was just one little problem. Bella's last message was going to be a bit harder to reply to!

If you want to check, turn back to page 97. You'll see that Bella sent *Lots of love*. Yuk! And she called herself *Bellz*. YUKKY YUK! And she even asked what James looked like. BLEURGHH! It was a good job there was only one more spelling club to go before the team was picked.

Here's the message I sent back to Bella. (And try not to laugh. I was doing it for Martha, remember?)

Dear Bella,

I'm very tall like you and I've got brown hair like you and I am very handsome with big muscles. So what words did you get today?

Love from James.

Dad was starting to wonder what was going on with all these messages. I told him I was just keeping Bella happy, which was true. After all, she was getting lovely messages from a very handsome James with big muscles. Ha ha, it's a good job she didn't know the truth!

Bella sent a message back the next day, so I got a pencil and paper ready to write the words down. But this is what it said . . .

Dear James,

You put LOVE FROM JAMES on the end! I'm so

happy! Have you got a girlfriend?

And call me Bellz!!!

LOTS of love Bellz xxx

EEEK! I didn't want to get into this girlfriend/boyfriend thing. I tried again ...

Dear Bellz,

You didn't tell me your spelling words! Please do because I think they are really interesting.

Love from James.

But here's what came back:

Dear James,

Tell me if you've got a girlfriend first.

OODLES OF LOVE from BELLZ xxx

Oh potties! Oh well, at least my next message didn't have any lies in it . . .

Dear Bellz,

No I haven't got a girlfriend.

I can't wait to know what words

you got!

Love from James.

Surely that HAD to be the last message I needed to send. I couldn't think of anything else I could put. I was calling her Bellz, I'd put *love from* and I told her James had got muscles and he wasn't married or anything.

But even if I'd run out of ideas,

117

Bella hadn't . . .

Dear James,

If you haven't got a girlfriend,

then you can put an X after your

messages if you like. I won't

mind!

LOVE AND HUGS BELLZ

XXXXX

I gave in. (Warning: the old man who

types these books out for me was

nearly sick when I told him about the next bit. It's so gross that you might want to read it with your eyes shut. Good luck!)

Dear Bellz,

I love you so much even more than spelling and I really hope you can be my girlfriend because you are so lovely especially if you tell me what spelling words you got in your last test.

Lots and lots and lots of love

from James XXXXXXXXXXX

I didn't have to wait long.

Dearest James,

I'd do anything for you . . .

OBSESSED,   INFATUATED,

BERSERK.

LOVE BELLZ XXXXXXXXX

XXXXXXXXXXXXXXXXXXXX

XXXXXXXXXXXXXXXXXXXX

XXXXXXXXXXXXXXXXXXXX

XXXXXXXXXXXXXXXXXXXX

XXXXXXXXXXXXXXXXXXXX

XXXXXXXXX . . .

. . . and all the XXXs filled up about three screens on the computer. **EEEKY FREAK!**

While I was copying the spelling words out, Dad was looking over my shoulder at the screen.

'What's all that about?' he asked.

'It's Bella's way of being nice and friendly,' I said.

'Yikes!' said Dad, then he did a little laugh. 'Your mum used to send me messages like that.'

'So what do we do?' I asked.

Dad pushed the DELETE button. The message disappeared for ever.

'It's for the best,' said Dad.

The Lesson

N ext day, when we got into lessons Miss Pingle was twiddling away on her computer.

'Settle yourselves down, children,' she said. 'I'm doing a little job for Mrs Twelvetrees.'

Ha ha! That's a joke.

Miss Pingle is a new teacher and there are lots of brilliant things about her. One of them is her hair which changes colour every week. (This week's colour = lemon. Crazy!)

About the only thing she isn't brilliant at is computers. She was pulling her serious face and wiggling the mouse, then she got up and went over to the printer in the corner. She clicked a switch on the wall, and stared at the printer hopefully.

Oh dear. The printer didn't do anything, but behind her the white board came on. As the screen slowly got brighter we could see she had been on the Internet.

'What's on the computer?' asked Ivy. 'Have you been buying something?'

'What?' said Miss P, then she noticed some fuzzy writing was appearing on the board. 'Oops! You're not meant to see that!'

She hurried back to the computer.

Click click twiddle! The screen went blank then the printer in the corner started buzzing.

'Yippee!' said Miss P. 'I've done it.'

She held her hand out and went along the front of the class giving everybody high fives. YO MISS PINGLE!

She got the piece of paper out of the printer, folded it up neatly and put it on her desk. I wondered if it was the spelling list?

'What's that?' asked Ivy.

'Private,' said Miss P.

Ha! It was *definitely* the spelling list.

'Now then, everybody,' said Miss Pingle. 'Today we're going to look at India.'

She pushed another button and the screen came on again, but it didn't look much like India. It looked more like a pair of long red boots in the sales for £24.99.

HA HA HA HA HA!

'That's not India!' we all shouted.

Poor Miss P started stabbing at the computer, but the boots stayed there.

'You'd look good in them,' said Ivy.

'Do you think so?' said Miss Pingle.

'Are you getting them?' asked Matty.

'Thinking about it,' admitted Miss P.

Just then the door opened and in

came Mrs Twelvetrees.

'Good morning gang!' said Mrs T.

'Good morning Mrs Twelvetrees,' said everybody.

Mrs T went over to Miss P who handed her the piece of folded paper.

'Thank you Miss Pingle,' said Mrs T, but then she looked up and saw what was on the white board.

'Miss Pingle!' she said crossly. 'Why have you got those boots on the board for £24.99?'

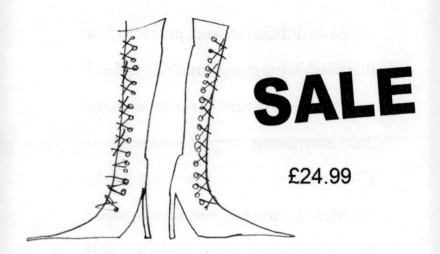

SALE

£24.99

'I'm sorry,' said Miss P. 'It was my mistake.'

'No. It was MY mistake,' said Mrs Twelvetrees.

130

Miss Pingle looked puzzled, but then Mrs T burst out laughing. 'Yes, I made a big mistake. I've got exactly the same boots myself and I paid £70!'

Mrs T headed off to the door but then turned back and waggled her piece of paper mysteriously. 'Martha? Ivy? I'll see you at lunchtime, chaps!'

Off she went and then India turned up on the board and we all found out where tea bags come from. How jolly interesting. They also do coffee and rice and curry stuff YUM! So let's have a round of applause for India clap clap clap.

Martha's Funny Mood

• •

At lunchtime we were all in the playground getting Ivy's leg ready for the spelling test. Ellie had Bianca's pen and the list of words, but Martha was being in a funny mood.

'It's not going to work,' said Martha.

133

'Why not?' I said. 'Ellie's all ready to do the writing, so we just need Ivy to pull her sock down . . .'

. . . and that's when I saw the problem. Ivy was wearing blue tights. **EEEK!**

But there's no stopping Ivy. She started wiggling like a worm in a frying pan.

'What ARE you doing?' I asked.

'I'm pulling my tights down of course,' said Ivy. 'Then Ellie can

134

write on my leg and I'll pull them up again.'

'So what happens in the test?' I asked. 'Are you going to pull your tights down again?'

'Why not?' said Ivy. 'Nobody will notice.'

But everybody in the whole playground had noticed! They had all stopped whatever they were doing and were looking our way.

'Thanks Ivy,' said Martha.

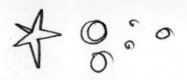

'But don't bother. I'm not going to spelling club.'

'Why not?' I said. 'There's a football match tonight. Don't you want to play?'

'Of course I do! But Gwendoline wants her pink laptop, and she deserves it more than me.'

'Why?' we all said. 'She's HORRIBLE!'

'Not as horrible as me,' said Martha. 'At least she's practised her spellings, but I'm cheating.'

'But you thought it was funny last time,' I said.

'That's because it didn't count then. But this time they're choosing the team so it's wrong.'

'Wrong? What's wrong?' said a voice behind us. It was Mrs Twelvetrees . . . **PANIC!**

She must have come out of the side door when we weren't looking. How much had she heard? Ellie was trembling so much, she dropped the list of words on the ground.

'Don't be dropping litter,' said Mrs T. 'Pick it up Ellie, and give it to me. I'll pop it in the library bin.'

Ellie blushed bright red like a tomato. What would happen if Mrs T saw the words on the paper? Ellie was so frozen in fear that she couldn't move.

'I'll get rid of it,' I said helpfully.

But before I could grab the list,

Mrs T stopped me.

'No!' said Mrs T. 'Ellie dropped it, so Ellie can pick it up.'

She stood there holding her hand out waiting for Ellie to give her the paper. It was awful. None of us knew what to do and then Ellie started to cry.

'Oh, golly,' said Mrs Twelvetrees. She sounded sorry. 'Don't get upset Ellie! One little piece of dropped paper isn't going to make the school fall down.'

Mrs Twelvetrees suddenly bent over and picked the paper up herself, then she stood there, twiddling it in her fingers.

'Chin up, chaps!' she said brightly. 'It's spelling club in five minutes, and

I'm choosing the team today.'

She waggled the paper in our faces.

'And you'll never guess what the star words are!' she said.

Then without thinking, she shoved the paper in her pocket and went back inside.

Ellie Makes Me Jealous

. . . .

Afternoon lessons were NOT a lot of fun.

Martha and Ivy hadn't gone to spelling club. What was the point? Martha was never going to get on the spelling team. Even worse, what would happen if Mrs Twelvetrees

142

found our list of star words in her pocket? Martha would be in such trouble that her mum would never ever let her play football again EVER. No wonder Martha spent the whole afternoon with her arms wrapped round her head.

It was almost as bad for Ellie. She sits next to Martha, and kept whispering 'sorry' to her and trying not to cry. Poor Ellie. All she'd done was drop a piece of paper, but it had ruined everything.

Finally we heard Motley ring the bell for end of school.

'Pack up your things, children,' said Miss Pingle. 'Leave your tables tidy!'

The boys all jumped up and charged out of the door like boys do. Martha got to her feet, wiped her nose on her sleeve and picked up her bag.

'Sorry Martha,' said Ellie. 'Sorry.

Sorry. Sorry sorry.'

Martha completely ignored her and didn't wait for any of us. She just pushed her way out of the classroom and went to get her coat, so Ivy and Bianca chased out after her to see if there was anything they could do. I was going with them but Ellie caught my sleeve. She had big red eyes where she'd been rubbing them.

'Agatha,' she said. 'Will you stay back with me?'

'What for?'

'I need to talk to Miss Pingle.'

Wow. Ellie is scared silly about talking to teachers. What was she going to say? Soon there were just the three of us in the classroom.

'Are you all right, Ellie?' asked Miss Pingle.

'Martha's upset,' said Ellie. 'It's all my fault.'

'Your fault?' asked Miss P. 'Why?'

'I copied some words off the board

146

that I shouldn't have,' said Ellie.

'What words?' said Miss P.

'When you printed out the spellings for Mrs Twelvetrees it came up on the board and I didn't know what it was so I just thought we had to write it down.'

What *was* Ellie talking about? I hadn't seen any words, it was too fuzzy. But did Miss Pingle know that?

'Oh no!' said Miss P. 'That was my silly fault. I turned the screen on by accident.'

'And I wrote it down,' said Ellie.

Suddenly I understood.

Goodness me Ellie Slippin! I thought to myself. *That is GENIUS!*

Ellie had just come up with a perfect explanation of how she came to be holding a list of the spelling words. If Mrs T found it, nobody would be in trouble. YO ELLIE! GOOD ONE! I so wish I'd thought of that. Cross

cross jealous jealous.

'So why is Martha upset?' asked Miss Pingle.

But Ellie was biting her lip and staring at the floor. She'd obviously been practising the first bit in her head, but that was as far as she'd got. Never mind, I could take it from there!

'Ellie showed us her bit of paper,' I said. 'But when Martha realised it was the spellings, she couldn't do the

test. Otherwise it would have been cheating.'

'Oh dear!' said Miss P. 'She should have just kept quiet about it.'

'Martha's far too honest. Her mum's going to go mad with her.'

'Why?'

'Because she's desperate for Martha to get on the spelling team. It could be nasty. She'll be waiting for Martha at the school gates right now.'

'Will she?' said Miss P already

hurrying towards the door.

'Big lady in a red coat,' I called out as Miss P shot off down the passage.

WAHOO! 10/10 and a gold sticker to Miss Pingle. She is going to get a big box of chocolates from me at the end of term. And I mean **SERIOUSLY** big.

Miss Pingle to the Rescue

After school the boys were going mad in the playground. They were warming up for the match by charging about with a football and being a **complete pain**. The worst one is Rory Bloggs who always runs with his head down, and bashes into everybody and everything WAM BASH DONK. We call him The Boy with the Ten Tonne Head. It's amazing the school has got any walls left after Rory's being playing ha ha!

The usual bunch of mums were hanging round by the gate, including Martha's mum in her big red coat. Ellie Slippin's mum was letting her have a hold of Ellie's baby sister Bubbles. Martha's mum was asking Bubbles some deep questions such as 'Who's a boot-i-ful likkoo girl then?' when Martha came out of the school door.

Usually Martha would chuck her bag down by the railings and get stuck in with the boys, but this time she didn't bother. Even when the ball rolled towards her, she didn't hoof it back. She just pushed past her mum, headed out of the gate and set off away up Odd Street.

Martha's mum couldn't go because she was still holding the baby, and that's when Miss Pingle came hurrying out of the door.

'Mrs Swan?' said Miss Pingle. 'I'm glad I caught you!'

'Oh dear,' said Martha's mum. 'Nothing serious I hope?'

'Oh no!' said Miss P. 'I just wanted to say how sorry we are that Martha isn't on the spelling team.'

'Isn't she?' asked Martha's mum.

'But she tried so hard!' said Miss P. 'It's my fault she didn't make it.'

'Your fault?'

'Oh yes,' said Miss Pingle. 'I accidentally showed her the list of words before the test, so Martha refused to take part. She said it would be unfair on the others.'

'Did she?' said Martha's mum. 'Did she really?'

'I know she's terribly disappointed,' said Miss P. 'But it was a very honest thing to do. You must be very proud of her.'

Martha's mum looked up the street where Martha was leaning against their front gate looking as sad as a wet cat.

'You say she's been trying hard?' asked Martha's mum.

'And she's been very honest,' said Miss P.

Guess what happened next?

I'll give you a clue. Martha's mum passed Bubbles back, then she quickly borrowed some money from Ivy's mum and charged off to the sports shop.

I toddled home and waited

because I knew that in about ten minutes' time there was going to be a loud banging on the door, and Martha would be standing there showing off her new football shirt. It was obvious because Martha's mum is really nice. All she had needed was the smallest excuse to let Martha off and play football again, so let's have a round of applause for Martha's big jolly mum clap clap clap. (Her first name is Irene by the way, but

she's a bit of a star so let's not be cheeky.)

So there I was waiting at home … and sure enough about ten minutes later there was a bang on the door. Ha ha, good old Martha! I went to the hall and took a deep breath. I knew Martha was going to give me a monster hug so I thought I'd better be ready. **Yahoo,** here we go!

I opened the door.

'I'm Bella,' said the girl.

Who?

. . . .

I slammed the door shut.

I was having the WEIRDEST daydream. Somehow I'd got this picture in my head of a girl outside our front door. She wasn't much bigger than Tilly, with curly blonde hair. She'd turned up with oodles of love and hugs, looking for James, and it wasn't the normal James either! She was expecting a tall, handsome version of James complete with muscles who would talk about spellings and then go on to give her three computer screens' worth of kisses. **EEEKY FREAK!**

I took a deep breath then let it out slowly.

Phew!

That felt better. I even started

to laugh a bit. Honestly, James with muscles? And spelling? And *kissing*? HA HA HA . . . *argh!*

There was another knock on the door.

Very carefully I opened it and this time I found myself face to face with a tummy.

It was a very slim tummy in a cream jumper. Looking down there was a short black skirt, long suntanned legs and shiny red high heels. Looking back up past the tummy, there was a chunky necklace, then high up on top was a face with big dark eyes and short black hair.

'You must be Agatha,' said the tall lady, and then she smiled and her mouth went right from one ear to the other and she had about 200 teeth. 'You won't remember me. I'm your mum's sister.'

'Auntie Zoe!' I gasped.

She was standing on our

doorstep at number 5 Odd Street just like she was posing for *The Duchess Catalogue*. It was **awesome!** What was even more awesome was the car parked out on the street behind her. I knew it had to be Auntie Zoe's because it was exactly the same colour

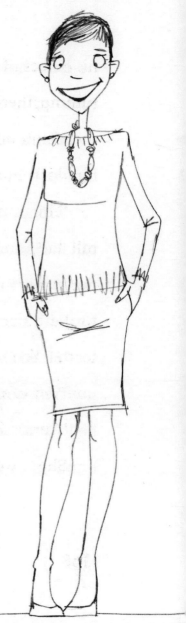

as her shoes! Matching shoes and cars is the sort of thing us models do.

There was a clumping noise of footsteps in the hallway behind me.

'Good grief!' gasped Dad. He put his hand up and stroked it across the top of his bald head a few times. I wasn't sure why.

'Hello there!' said Auntie Z.

'Yes gosh hello and hello gosh hello yes,' said Dad. He stroked his hand across his head again. Then mum appeared behind him.

'Zoe!' she blurted out, and immediately pushed past Dad and me and gave Auntie Z a big rough hug that nearly pulled her off her shoes. 'What brings you here?'

'Filming down the high street,' said Zoe.

'Oh WOW!' I said. 'Are you an actress?'

'Hardly!' said Auntie Z. 'I just sat at the back of a bank pretending to be a secretary for an advert.'

'You look fabulous!' giggled Mum.

'I'm glad you think so,' said Auntie Z. 'It took me three hours to get like this. And if I can borrow your bathroom it'll take me two minutes to look like a scarecrow again.'

'Come in, come in!' said Mum.

'I hope you don't mind, but we didn't know we were coming this way until today.'

'We?' I said. 'Is there somebody else?'

'Of course,' said Auntie Zoe. 'I've brought Bella to meet you.'

Auntie Zoe stepped past me, and sitting on the fence behind her was the girl with blonde curls. Although she was small, when I got a better look at her I realised she was at least as old as me. 'Who are you?' she demanded suspiciously.

'Agatha.'

'But you're supposed to be pretty,' she said.

Well honestly. Of all the cheek!

This is the girl who told James that she had brown hair and was the tallest in her class! You just can't trust some people.

Then I remembered my really nasty thought. James was supposed to be tall and handsome with muscles! What was she going to say when she saw him?

I didn't have to wait long to find out because James came down the street bouncing a football. He just pushed past Bella and me and went in.

'Is that James?' she gasped.

Well, there was no point lying, was there?

'Yes,' I said.

'Oh no!' she said looking horrified.

'What's the matter with you?' I asked.

'He's . . . he's . . . *gorgeous*!'

'James? Gorgeous?' I said.

'He's so tall. And handsome. And with muscles!' said Bella. 'What's he going to think of me?'

She looked really upset. I found myself feeling a bit sorry for her, she was obviously **completely bonkers.**

'Don't worry,' I said. 'He's a bit shy.'

'Shy? You're kidding!' said Bella.

176

'You should see what he puts in his emails.'

'He's VERY shy about emails,' I said. 'Best not to mention them.'

'Oh,' said Bella sounding disappointed. 'Never mind. At least we can talk about spelling.'

'NO!' I shouted by accident. 'I mean, no, he's even more shy about spelling.'

'So what can we talk about?' asked Bella.

'It's probably best just to look at him,' I said. 'You can admire his handsome muscles.'

'OK,' said Bella with a big happy smile.

Yes, she was as bonkers as a box of conkers. No wonder I was getting to like her.

Don't Talk About the Nappy

. . . .

Teatime with Auntie Zoe and Bella was surprisingly brilliant! We were in a bit of a rush because James had to get off to football, so Mum sent Dad out to get some emergency tea. He came back with 'A Real Taste of Spain' which had juicy prawns, rice, peas and an exciting blend of herbs. Each serving also had 322 calories, 11 grams of fat and 1240 mgs of sodium (no, I still don't know what that is). But the best thing is that Dad

got TWO boxes.

That was enough for eight people, but there were only seven of us, so we each got an extra blob of fat and a few more mgs of sodium

YUM!

Auntie Zoe and Mum did all the talking. Tilly stared at Bella who stared at James who stared at Dad . . . and Dad kept staring at Auntie Zoe and stroking the top of his head.

Eventually I had to ask.

'Dad, why do you keep stroking your head?'

'I don't,' said Dad stroking his head.

'Yes you do,' laughed Mum. 'You're combing your hair to look nice for Zoe.'

'But I haven't got a comb!' said Dad.

'You haven't got any hair,' said Tilly which was a bit unkind. But it was only Dad so who cares?

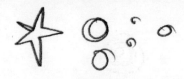

HA HA HA HA HA!

'Last time we saw Zoe he had some hair,' said Mum. 'And now we've seen her again, Dad's forgotten it's all gone.'

'He had lovely hair,' said Auntie Zoe. 'Long and shiny with beautiful curls.'

HA HA HA HA HA!

For some reason Dad WITH hair is even funnier than Dad without hair.

'I remember he was taking my photograph,' said Auntie Zoe. 'Agatha was a baby on my knee and I was wearing a light blue dress, and her nappy came undone . . .'

WHAT? Now that is NOT funny. Grrr.

'LOOK AT THE TIME!' I said a bit too loudly, and immediately started putting all the plates in the sink. 'We have to get to James's football match.'

'Oh dear,' said Mum to Auntie Zoe. 'You've only just got here.'

'Maybe we could come along and watch too?' said Auntie Zoe.

So that's what they did.

The Battle of Odd Green

· ·

It was cold, it was muddy and after a **WHOLE HOUR** of kicking and shouting, it was still nil–nil.

YAWN! But that's football for you.

Motley the caretaker had set

the goals up on Odd Green after school, and then he'd spent the game running around the pitch trying to keep out of the way. It took me ages to realise he was supposed to be the referee, but he'd given up blowing his whistle because nobody did what he said. Poor old Motley!

At least Martha was getting to play along with James on the blues' team. She'd turned up with her mum before the game, and when she

showed off her new football shirt, everybody had cheered.

'And DON'T get it dirty,' Martha's mum had shouted.

But everybody knows that a muddy Martha is a happy Martha. Sure enough, about four and a half seconds later, a boy on the yellow team had deliberately banged into her, and they'd both gone over. He rolled about on the ground moaning and clutching his leg, while Martha got straight back up with a big smile, all ready to take on the next one. **WAHOO GO MARTHA!** We love Martha.

Dad had joined a bunch of noisy blue team dads who were all pointing and shouting at the game. Mum and Auntie Zoe weren't even pretending to watch, they were still yakking away like mental. Tilly was stomping about in her wellies looking for worms to squash, which just left me standing with Bella. She'd spent the whole time watching James and doing little waves at him whenever he came close.

I should have guessed what was coming.

'James hasn't waved back once,' she said. 'And he didn't talk to me at teatime.'

'Really?' I said trying to sound surprised.

'Do you think James likes me?' said Bella.

'Oh yes, I'm sure he does,' I said.

'Do you think he likes me a lot?'

'It's always hard to tell with

James,' I said. 'He doesn't show his feelings much. He's the quiet type.'

And then suddenly . . .

'GOAL!' shouted everybody.

Although I hadn't been watching, it wasn't hard to guess who'd scored.

James was jumping up and down cheering, then he stood there with his arms outstretched while all the others came to give him a big BOY HUG. He ran round giving

them all high fives, and finally he

charged across in front of us

beating his chest with his

fists shouting WAY-OH

WAY-OH WAY-OH.

'The quiet type?' moaned Bella. 'He's not the quiet type! Why didn't he do that when he saw me?'

'Ah, well, he does like his football,' I said.

'He obviously likes it more than he likes me,' said Bella sadly. 'He's got a heart of mud.'

She went quiet again. Oh dear. She might have been bonkers but I was starting to feel rotten about the emails I'd sent.

(By the way, you just went past the title of the book. Did you notice it? If you did then have a gold star and a little cheer WAHOO!)

When the game started again, the yellow dads did some extra loud shouting, and the yellow team woke up a bit. At one point there was a yellow waiting quite near the blues' goal when the ball came flying over to him. Martha was too far away to do anything, but Rory Bloggs was

close. He put his big head down and charged.

'WAAAAAH!' shouted Rory.

His head hit the yellow boy in the tummy and knocked him over.

'Ha ha ha!' laughed all the blues.

'PENALTY!' shouted all the yellow dads at Motley.

'Is it?' said Motley. 'Hang on, then.'

Motley had put his whistle in his pocket to keep it warm, but by the

time he'd got it out, a yellow had already taken the penalty kick and the score was 1–1.

Now BOTH teams had woken up, and things were getting rougher.

Two big yellows were on the attack, but Martha banged into one of them and sent him flying. That just left the other yellow to face Rory, so Rory did what Rory does.

'WAAAAAH!' shouted The Boy with the Ten Tonne Head.

But this time the yellow knew what to expect. As Rory came charging towards him, the yellow skipped aside. Rory missed and shot off the pitch and went head first into a tree. THUNK!

Rory sat on the ground looking very dizzy. There was no way he could play any more, so the blues looked around to see if they had anyone to take his place. All the spare people had got so bored with the start of the game they'd gone home, so James ended up looking at me, but NO WAY! Then he saw Bella doing her little wave at him.

'What do you want?' demanded James.

'Just saying hello,' said Bella.

'Yeah, whatever,' said James. 'We need somebody who can play.'

'OK!' she shouted and ran on to the pitch.

There was a bit of an argument about it, but Bella wasn't backing down.

'I go jogging with Mum,' said Bella. 'So I bet I can run faster than any of you lot.'

The blues all turned to stare at

Auntie Zoe who looked like she could run at 100 mph.

'It would help me,' said Martha. 'Even if she just fills the gap where Rory was.'

So Bella borrowed Rory's shirt, and pulled it on over her top.

'You stay at the back with Martha,' said James. 'If the ball comes over, don't be clever. Just try to kick it to one of us.'

When the yellows saw great big

Martha walking back into position with the little person running alongside her, they all burst out laughing.

'Ignore them,' said Martha. 'They're only boys.'

Motley blew his whistle and the game started again.

Tinky tonk
Tiddly plop

Tick tock

Went the clock . . .

But then suddenly there was a good bit! The ball landed by Martha. Two yellows came charging over, so Martha ran off keeping the ball close to her feet. The yellows chased after her, but when they realised she was too big and too quick for them, they threw themselves forwards and grabbed on to her shirt. Martha kept

205

going and pulled them both over.
Her shirt was stretching and
stretching . . . and then a loud voice
drowned out everything else on the
pitch –

'HEY, YOU TWO!'
screamed Martha's mum. 'GET
YOUR HANDS OFF
THAT NEW SHIRT!'

But they didn't let go and Martha
didn't stop running.

Martha's mum put two fingers

206

in her mouth and made a huge loud whistle noise. Everybody stopped and looked at Martha's mum.

'IF YOU TWO DON'T LET GO, I'M SENDING YOU OFF!' she shouted.

Motley came running over.

'Did you whistle?' he demanded. 'You're not allowed to whistle. I'm in charge.'

'Oh are you?' said Martha's mum. 'Then if that shirt gets ripped,

you'll be the one mending it!'

'I warn you madam!' said Motley. 'Any more talk like that and I'll pack the goals away.'

Now everyone was staring at Motley and starting to laugh. In the meantime the ball had rolled away and was sitting on its own in the middle of the pitch. I ran down the side to get close to where Bella was standing.

'The referee hasn't blown his

whistle,' I told her. 'So the game's still going!'

Bella ran off like a bullet

WHIZZ!

She'd got the ball halfway to the goal before the yellows had realised what was happening. Everyone suddenly charged after her, but she was miles ahead.

'Pass it!' shouted James trying to catch up. 'Leave it to me!'

Bella completely ignored him.

There was only the yellow goalkeeper in front of her. He saw her coming and came out to dive on the ball, but Bella was moving so fast that he completely missed. She just ran straight on into the goal with the ball rolling along in front of her.

WAHOO GO BELLA!
BIG HUGS AND HIGH
FIVES!

The Ending

· ·

It was late by the time we got home, so Auntie Zoe and Bella had to get going quite quickly.

We were all standing out by the car. Bella was ready to go, but Auntie Zoe is an auntie. The rules for aunties state that you can't leave until you've given everybody a big hug.

First she hugged James which was funny because he got a lipsticky mark on his cheek. Even if your auntie is Auntie Zoe, a lipsticky mark from your auntie is NOT COOL ha ha love it love it!

All the time she was hugging James, Dad was stroking his head so he was all ready for his big hug. Ha ha! Nice try dad, and he did get a very big hug but NO lipstick. Aw poor Dad! Boo hoo hoo.

Normally Tilly runs and hides from things like auntie hugs, but for Auntie Zoe she'd climbed on to the wall so she was all ready for it.

I got the best hug because Auntie Zoe whispered to me that she was doing a fitness DVD and maybe maybe MAYBE I could be in it! Wahoo, I might be famous. Pass the champagne darling *slurp, burp* *WEEEEE!*

And then Auntie Zoe gave Mum
a hug and they both started crying.

But all this hugging wasn't the most exciting thing happening out on Odd Street that night! Just as they were driving off, I saw Bella give James a shy little wave through the car window . . . and James did a little wave back! Crazy times.

So we all went inside, and Mum took me and Tilly upstairs to get sorted out for bedtime and school tomorrow and putting socks and pants in the wash and all that stuff.

I was just coming down to get a glass of water when I heard James's voice in the living room talking to Dad.

'You know cousin Bella?' said James. 'I just remembered, she sent me an email. Do you think it's too late to send a reply?'

It was WAY too late James!

'Er . . . that depends,' said Dad. 'What did you want to say?'

'Nothing much,' said James. 'Just being nice and friendly.'

Now this is **VERY** private. I don't want you laughing at James. He might be a boy and horrible and all that, but sometimes he does things right. You can only read this if you promise not to laugh or tell anybody.

Promise?

OK, here it is:

Hi Bella,

Thanks for being on our team. It was a really good goal. Matty says that I have to ask if you'll come and play for us again. I hope so. Good luck with stuff.

Love from James

Gosh how exciting! I know what you're thinking.

Will James and Bella ever meet again?

Will they get married?

Will they go and live in a little cottage by the seaside?

Will he go bald?

Will she get hairy legs?

Will they have 10000000 kids?

Will they all look like James, even the girls?

URGH!

What a horrible thought to end the story with, but don't worry! I promised Bianca I'd put her zebra facts at the back of the book, so at least that'll take your mind off it and leave you with nice thoughts ha ha!

But right now, you have a choice. As the story has finished you can EITHER have the normal ending like this . . .

THE END

. . . OR if you think that's just a little bit boring you can go for the mega bonkers BELLA sort of ending. It's over the page, so are you ready?

Take a deep breath and here we go . . .

THANK YOU my **DARLING READER** for reading my little story!

OODLES and **DOODLES** of **LOVE** and **HUGS** to **YOU** for ever and ever and **EVER.**

See you soooooooon!

XXXXXXXXXXXXXXXXXX

XXXXXXXXXXXXXXXXXX

XXXXXXXXXXXXXXXXXXX

XXXXXXXXXXXXXXXXXX

XXXXXXXXXXXXXXXXXX

XXXXXXXXXXXXXXXXXXXX

. . . . *pause for breath* . . . .

XXXXXXXXXXXXXXXXXXX

XXXXX

(I think all books
should end like
that, especially
school books ha
ha wicked!)

Bianca's Facts About Zebras

Bianca told me about a million zebra facts, so these are just a few of them, and I put in a WRONG fact for fun!

Can you guess which one I made up?

1) There are three different types of zebra and they all live in Africa.